# POWER HITTER

# POWER HITTER

M. G. *Higgins*

MINNEAPOLIS

Darby Creek
A division of Lerner Publishing Group, Inc.
241 First Avenue North
Minneapolis, MN 55401 U.S.A.

Website address: www.lernerbooks.com

The images in this book are used with the permission of:
© Kelpfish/Dreamstime.com, p. 117; © iStockphoto.com/
Jill Fromer p. 120 (banner background); © iStockphoto
.com/Naphtalina, pp. 120, 121, 122 (brick wall
background). Front cover: © Erik Isakson/CORBIS.
Back cover: © Kelpfish/Dreamstime.com.

Main body text set in Janson Text 12/17.5.
Typeface provided by Adobe Systems.


Higgins, M. G.
        Power hitter / by M.G. Higgins.
            p.   cm. — (Travel team)
        ISBN: 978–0–7613–8324–6 (lib. bdg. : alk. paper)
        [1. Baseball—Fiction.]  I. Title.
    PZ7.H5349554Po  2012
    [Fic]—dc23                                    2011022573

Manufactured in the United States of America
1—BP—12/31/11

"The way a team plays as a whole determines its success. You may have the greatest bunch of individual stars in the world, but if they don't play together, the club won't be worth a dime. "

—BABE RUTH

# CHAPTER 1

Sammy Perez's palms were slimed with sweat. He was thankful for his batting gloves. The last thing he needed was for his hands to slip. Taking a deep breath, he strode back to the box. He tapped the plate twice, took another practice swing, and shook his head. The bat's balance still seemed off. The weight was all wrong. Nothing about wooden bats felt right! He pictured himself having a Little-League hissy fit and running home to Mom.

*Perez, you wuss,* Sammy scolded himself. *Get a grip.* Sammy was usually one of the best hitters on the Roadrunners, an elite traveling team from Las Vegas. *Usually.*

Taking another deep breath, Sammy eyed the infield. Gus Toomey had a short lead off second, holding his hands out as if to say, *Come on, dude, hit it already!* On the mound, Carson Jamison squinted and waved off a sign. But there was no question which pitch was coming. And Carson was such a Picasso; he'd paint it right where he wanted it.

Uncomfortable or not, Sammy had to try for a hit. He raised his bat, settling into his stance. Carson nodded, wound up, and fired. Yep, it was the high and tight heater Sammy expected. He swung and connected, but the ball *clunked* off the thin handle, dribbling right back to Carson for an easy third out to first.

"Crap!" Sammy yelled, not even bothering to run. He threw the wooden bat as far as he could down the third baseline.

Gus nudged Sammy's shoulder as he trotted off the field. "Calm down, dude. You'll get the hang of it."

"Ya think?" Sammy followed Gus into the dugout. "I'm a power hitter, and I can't hit. This really sucks."

Scott Harris, the Roadrunners' coach, walked calmly into the dugout carrying Sammy's bat. Sammy hesitated before taking it from him. In typical Coach Harris style, he silently crossed his arms over his chest, waiting for Sammy to admit his mistake. Even though Coach was gray-haired and in his fifties, he was as fit and energetic as a drill sergeant.

Sammy's hot temper usually cooled off quickly under that glare, but his face still felt hot. "Sorry," he said. "I shouldn't have thrown the bat."

"No, you shouldn't," Coach said. "This is your first day using wood, and I'm not expecting miracles. Work with Wash on your form and then practice in the cage until you're comfortable."

Sammy reached down for his glove. He didn't know how much working with Assistant

Coach Washington would really help him at this point. Sammy knew he was risking Coach's wrath, but he had to say *something*. "Coach, do you really think switching to a wooden tournament is a good idea? I mean, that's a pitch I get on base with nine times out of ten with a composite." He heard feet shuffling and a few murmurs. Most of the Runners were in the dugout listening instead of going back on the field.

"Do I have to remind you why we're participating in this tournament?" Coach's voice was low, but his words were crisp.

Sammy closed his eyes for a second. He could still hear the sound of TJ's jaw cracking from the hard comebacker. Any higher and the ball would have fractured his skull and probably killed him. As it was, TJ's face was wired up for months. He was an ace pitcher with a great future. But the injury freaked him and his parents, and he quit playing ball.

Sammy noticed some of his teammates had crossed their arms like Coach Harris. Carson, a good friend of TJ's, glowered at Sammy.

Tension was thick between pitchers and some infielders, who wanted to avoid injuries, and power hitters like Sammy who were afraid they'd never make it to the pros or to a good college without that aluminum pop and bigger sweet spot.

This wasn't the time to argue. "No, Coach," Sammy said. "You don't have to remind me."

"Good." Coach uncrossed his arms and announced to the team, "We'll be practicing with *only* wooden bats before the Austin tournament, which is a week from Friday. And no excuses about the equipment. These are the best professional bats on the market."

"Thanks to my dad," Carson added.

Coach nodded. "Which Mr. Jamison has generously donated." He looked around the dugout, his eyes wide. "Well, what are you standing around for? Get out there!"

Sammy trudged to his position in right field. He'd never dreaded playing ball before. But he had a really bad feeling about this tournament.

# CHAPTER 2

Sammy was thankful he didn't have another at bat that practice. The embarrassment of again not getting a hit would have killed him. In the dugout, he shoved his equipment into his bag. Nellie Carville, Carlos "Trip" Costas, and Darius McKay, three of the team's best hitters, headed for the batting cages with wooden bats tucked under their arms.

"Joining us?" asked Wash, the Runners'

assistant coach. Wash's baseball roots dated back to a granddad who played in the Negro Leagues. He was a great hitting coach, but Sammy wasn't in the mood for *any* coaching right now.

"No. I'll practice at home."

Wash raised one of his bushy eyebrows.

"What?" Sammy asked, his temper flaring again. He was one of the hardest-working players on the team, and it really annoyed him when someone hinted otherwise.

"Okay," Wash said, holding up his hands. "Do what you need to do. Try not to overthink it." He marched off to the batting cages.

Sammy grabbed a couple of wooden bats from the rack, hoping his dad had fixed his broken pitching machine.

"Need a lift?" Gus asked.

"Yes. Thank you."

"*De nada.*"

Sammy smirked. "Enough with the Spanish."

"I need the practice," Gus said as they walked across the parking lot. "*Español* is my worst class, and I want to use it over the summer so I don't forget. Anyway, you owe me for all the rides."

"Like you can't afford it." Sammy instantly wished he could stuff the words back in his mouth. "Sorry. I didn't mean it."

"That was low. But I get it. It's the wooden bat thing. Dragging you down, man."

"Well, yeah. I *smoked* the Albuquerque Regional last season. Ten ribbies, two home runs, including a grand slam."

"Yeah, I was there, remember?"

"And it was crawling with scouts. Now we're switching to this lame wooden tournament instead. Unbelievable."

"Scouts will be there too."

"Exactly. They'll have front-row seats for Sammy's fail."

"Dude, dude." Gus shook his head. His BMW roadster beeped as he unlocked it with the remote key. "What you need is a diversion."

Sammy froze with his hand on the door handle. He knew what was coming. "No parties. No girls. We're in training."

"Dude, we're not in training to be monks. Loosen up."

Sammy shook his head as he sat on the soft leather passenger seat. The door made a solid *foomp* sound when he closed it, totally unlike his pickup's cheap rattle. The pickup wasn't even really his. His uncle loaned it to him, when it ran. Which it didn't at the moment. Taking a deep sniff of the leather and new-car smell, Sammy imagined buying a car like this. Right after he turned pro and built his family a ten-bedroom house.

"So." Gus started the car, which purred softly. "There's this girl . . ."

Sammy rolled his eyes and groaned.

"You will like her, amigo. Her name is Kelsey. She's a friend of Olivia's—"

"What part of *we are in training* do you not understand?" Sammy interrupted. "I have to keep my stats up. We're in 17 and under now. People are paying closer attention."

"Yo, dude! Listen to yourself. Man does not live by baseball alone."

"Easy for you to say."

Gus put the car in reverse. "Man, chill out, will ya?"

Sammy whacked his knuckles against his forehead. "Sorry. Again." He flopped his head back against the leather headrest. "But you have to admit, Augustus Toomey has a lot more career opportunities than Samuel Perez. I *need* baseball."

"If you say so." Gus turned right out of the parking lot, toward Sammy's neighborhood. "Although, have you taken a good look in the mirror lately? According to Olivia, you have that tall, dark, and handsome thing going on."

"Whatever, man."

"True. Kelsey is dying to meet you. So . . . you, me, Olivia, and Kelsey. This Saturday. I'll work out the details."

"No."

"Cool. It's a date." Gus punched Sammy's arm.

"Hey!" Sammy swatted at Gus's hand and couldn't help laughing. He and Gus were so different. Sammy wasn't sure why they were friends. Sammy's family struggled financially, and Gus's dad was one of the richest men in Vegas. But then, all of the Roadrunners came from different high schools, towns, and backgrounds. Sammy was just grateful he had at least one friend on the team.

It only took a few minutes to reach Sammy's block, three miles from the ballpark. Sammy's family had moved into a new development about five years ago. The house was small, with only three bedrooms, but Sammy's parents wanted to raise their four kids in a safe neighborhood. Sammy knew his parents were struggling to pay for the house. The neighborhood was dotted with foreclosure signs. Some of those houses had been empty for months. It gave the entire block a spooky, deserted feel. Sammy couldn't wait to move his family out of here.

"I think your dad is home," Gus said.

Up ahead, Sammy saw a sleek black limo in the driveway. The car wasn't theirs, of course. It belonged to casino director Alexander Jamison, who also happened to be the father of Carson, the team's star pitcher and all-around jerk of a guy. Sammy's dad worked for the senior Jamison as a chauffeur. "I guess Dad's working tonight. He brings the car home when he has a few hours to kill before he picks up Jamison."

"It's a nice ride."

Sammy snickered. "I wouldn't know."

"You've never been inside?"

"Nope. Against the rules."

"Dude," Gus said as Sammy got out of his car. "How would Jamison ever know if you set foot in his car?"

"It doesn't matter. *I'd* know."

Gus opened his mouth to say something, and then seemed to change his mind. "Need a lift to practice tomorrow?"

Sammy hesitated. "No, thanks. I've got it covered."

"*Bueno. Hasta linguini.*" Gus flashed Sammy a peace sign and sped off.

Sammy took a deep breath. Although he really needed the batting practice, part of him hoped his dad hadn't gotten around to fixing his pitching machine.

# CHAPTER 3

Sammy could see his dad hunched over his workbench through the open garage door. "Hey, Dad," Sammy called. He leaned the wooden bats against a couple of sawhorses

"Hey." Tony Perez didn't look up from the throwing arm he was repairing. He'd grown a slight paunch in his middle age, but otherwise Sammy guessed his dad was as trim as when he played on the Florida Marlins' Dominican farm team. A Miami newspaper article with his photo still hung above the workbench: "Best Year Yet for Promising Dominican Sluggers." Sammy had read the article so many times he'd practically memorized it. Next to the article was a photo of fellow Dominican Sammy Sosa. It was autographed by the famous Cubby himself. Sosa was his dad's favorite player and Sammy's namesake.

"How many hits today?" his dad asked, still focused on his repair job.

"None."

His dad looked up, eyebrows raised.

"We're using those," Sammy said, pointing at the wooden bats. He explained the team's switch from the Albuquerque tournament to the wooden tournament in Austin. As he spoke, his dad's frown deepened and a crease formed between his eyes.

"That's not fair," his dad said when Sammy was done talking. "You've trained with aluminum all your life. And they expect you to switch *now*? You've been building momentum, Sammy. Every tournament counts this year!" His dad's face was red.

"I know. Don't have a heart attack."

His dad leapt off of his stool and pulled out his cell phone. "I'll talk to Coach Harris."

"No! You'll just embarrass me. Anyway, who do you think is behind this?"

His dad's eyes unfocused as Sammy's words sank in. Sammy's dad had seen what happened to TJ. He shoved the phone back in his pocket and slumped onto his stool. "The pitchers."

"Right. Especially your boss's son."

His dad grabbed a screwdriver and stabbed it into the top of the wooden workbench.

"Dad, don't worry about it. This isn't your problem."

He glared at Sammy. "I haven't supported your baseball career all these years for you to fall short now. You need that big sweet spot, Sammy. You're a power hitter. It's what you do."

Sammy agreed with his dad, but this wasn't solving anything. He pointed at the workbench. "How's the pitching machine?"

"I'll have it fixed by tomorrow. It's a piece of crap. We should have bought the X-600."

"Too expensive."

His dad yanked the screwdriver out of the tabletop. "This isn't right, Sammy. What happened to TJ was terrible, but it was an accident. Could have just as easily happened with a wooden bat. It was just one of those things."

Sammy could practically see the memory that was running through his dad's head. His dad had been days away from being called up to the big leagues when his knee gave out rounding second base. He was trying to turn a double into a triple. The knee eventually healed, but he wasn't as fast afterwards, and the Marlins wouldn't sign him. No team would take a chance. *It was just one of those things* was his dad's mantra.

"Sammy!" Thomás, Sammy's six-year-old brother, ran into the garage.

"Hey, T-Rex." Sammy grabbed him under the arms and lifted him off the cement floor.

Thomás curled his fingers into pretend claws. "*Grrrrrrr.* I will eat you."

"Not if I eat you first." Sammy pretended to bite his nose and then set him down.

His mom lumbered into the garage, carrying Sammy's two-year-old sister, Felicia. They both looked wilted and ready to collapse. "Outdoor summer camp in Las Vegas should be outlawed."

"Hi, Mom."

"Hi, sweetie. You look so handsome in your training outfit. You remind me of your dad more and more every day." She winked. "How was practice?"

"Practice was . . . fine." Sammy exchanged a glance with his dad. They wouldn't tell her about his baseball problems. She had enough on her plate with her job and taking care of four kids.

She set Felicia down and led her by the hand toward the kitchen door. "Is Marlena home yet?"

"Still working," Dad said. Sammy's sixteen-year-old sister had a summer job at the mall.

His mom disappeared into the kitchen with Felicia and Thomás in tow.

Sammy's dad focused back on the Super Pitch X-400. He was repairing it because he couldn't afford a new one. His chauffeur pay wasn't bad, but the cost for Sammy to play on the Roadrunners' elite traveling team was incredible: uniforms, membership fees, airfare, the best equipment. Where would his family be living right now if it weren't for Sammy? They all sacrificed so he could play ball. Sammy took a deep breath. He owed them everything. He would make it up to them.

As he turned to follow his mom inside, his dad said, "Sammy."

Sammy stopped. "What?"

"I . . . uh . . . finally got that guy's number. The sports-medicine doc I told you about. He was in the limo on Monday. He says there are some new products out there. Safe. They can't be detected on tests."

"Dad—"

"Look, I know it's not a perfect solution. But if you're going to be using wood more, it will give you an edge."

Sammy took another deep breath. PEDs. The idea of using performance-enhancing drugs made his stomach clench. But if he couldn't hit with wooden bats, he would need an edge.

"It's your call," his dad said. "Let me know."

Sammy nodded and walked slowly into the house.

# CHAPTER 4

Sammy stood in his position in right field, pounding his fist in his glove. Danny Manuel, the Runners' usual center fielder, was in the process of hitting a string of foul balls. It was a boring practice, but Sammy was at least relieved that other players were also having problems hitting with wooden bats. Maybe it would convince Coach to switch back to the Albuquerque tournament.

Sweat dripped down Sammy's face. It was the end of June and broiling. Like he often did, he imagined getting drafted by a team with a cooler climate—the Colorado Rockies, the Seattle Mariners, the San Diego Padres. The average temp in San Diego was seventy degrees. He'd looked it up online. Felicia and Thomás could spend their summers at SeaWorld. Marlena could shop at the mall instead of working there. His mom could lie on the beach all day. His dad could . . . well, his dad could do anything he wanted. Like plant flowers in their two-acre landscaped garden, with its fishpond and fountain and. . . .

*CRACK.*

It took a second for the sound to register in Sammy's brain. A hardball making contact with a wooden bat was worlds different from the aluminum *ping* he was used to. And *Danny* had hit it that hard? He wasn't exactly known for his strength. Throwing off a twinge of jealousy, Sammy focused on the ball. It was flying fast in his direction, veering toward the right-center alley. Gauging the ball's speed and height, Sammy turned and sprinted. While still racing across the grass, he looked up, eyed the ball during the last few seconds of its downward arc, and made a backhanded grab. Then he twisted and threw on his back foot to the infield.

Gus whistled his approval at first base. Sammy shrugged. What he wanted was another chance at bat. He'd struck out his first time up. If Danny could hit the ball that hard, why couldn't he?

Coach Harris swatted Sammy's butt as he trotted off the field. "Big-league catch, Sammy."

"Thanks." Sammy quickly shoved on his batting gloves and helmet. He was up second and wanted to fit in as many practice swings as he could on deck.

Danny sneered at Sammy as he left the dugout for the field. "Thanks for robbing me of a double."

Sammy grabbed Danny's arm and stopped him. "How did you do that?"

"Do what?"

"Make contact. You really slammed it."

"You're asking *me* for batting advice?" Danny laughed. "I don't know. I just hit it." He trotted out to his position.

Sammy took a deep breath and picked a wooden bat from the rack. He swung it loosely in the on-deck circle. The bat felt heavy. Awkward. *It shouldn't matter,* he told himself. *A big leaguer should be able to get on base with a lead pipe or a carrot stick.*

"Listen, Sammy," Wash said, leaning against the dugout railing. "Wood doesn't swing as fast. That means you can't spend all day watching pitches to make last-minute adjustments. Get the bat off your shoulder faster."

Sammy nodded. It made sense. Except analyzing pitches was one of the skills that made him a good power hitter. He fine-tuned his swing just at the last second. And Wash was saying he couldn't do that anymore? Great. He rolled his shoulders.

Darius fouled out, and Sammy walked up to the plate. Maybe if he used his instincts instead of thinking too much. But his instincts caused him to swing and miss three of Carson's fastballs in quick succession. One of them was right over the plate.

"Crap!" Sammy yelled after the third strike.

Carson snickered.

Sammy glared at Carson and marched into the dugout. After jamming his bat into the rack, he drop-kicked his helmet into the locker room and almost bumped into Coach Harris on his way out. "Sorry," Sammy said. "I shouldn't have kicked my helmet. I shouldn't have yelled."

"Work with Wash. We need you hitting, not striking out."

Sammy threw his hands in the air. "I know!" He plopped onto the dugout bench.

"Cool it, Sammy! I don't like hotheads and neither do big-league teams."

That cooled down Sammy more than anything else Coach could have said. The heat drained from his face. He took a deep breath. "I'm sorry. I was out of line." He jiggled his knees. "No one's going to draft me after this wooden tournament, anyway." Then, using his most reasonable voice, he said, "Are you absolutely sure this is a good idea, Coach? Is there any way we can switch back to Albuquerque?"

"We're already committed to Austin. Work with Wash, like I said. He'll help you make some adjustments. The team is counting on you, Sammy. We need your big bat out there. If you'd just—"

Coach Harris was interrupted by a *crack* out on the field. But it wasn't the satisfying sound of a hardball making contact with a bat. It was the sound of splintering wood.

# CHAPTER 5

G us stared with wide eyes at the broken half of a bat in his hands. The other half had shot through the air toward third base, where Trip was fielding while Nellie batted. If Trip hadn't jumped back at the last second, it could have stabbed his throat. He gasped. "Holy crap."

Wash trotted onto the field. "You okay?"

Trip nodded, but he looked shaken.

"Wooden bats break," Wash announced to

everyone. "You know this."

"But it happened so fast," Trip said.

"Which is why you need to constantly stay alert."

"Yeah, you lazy punks," Carson muttered from the pitcher's mound. "Now you know what it's like to face aluminum comebackers every day."

Trip strode toward Carson, rolling his fingers into fists. "So, what, you pitchers want us to get stabbed by wooden stakes to prove a point?"

The dugout emptied. All the pitchers and the players who were in favor of wood surrounded Carson. Trip's friends gathered around third base. Sammy hung back near home plate with Gus. Sammy didn't like Carson, but he wasn't a big friend of Trip's, either. He just hoped this would put a few doubts in Coach's mind about the wooden tournament.

"Break it up!" Coach yelled, joining Wash on the field. They held out their arms, separating the two groups. "Practice is over!

This better not happen again or there's going to be some serious benching!"

The team slowly walked off the field. But instead of going to the dugout, Carson swerved toward Sammy, stopping inches from his face. "This has something to do with you, doesn't it?" His breath smelled like old cheese.

"What are you talking about?"

"You can't hit wood, so you're trying to talk Coach into switching to the old tournament."

"Get out of my face." Sammy shoved Carson's shoulder.

Carson raised his hands and slammed Sammy's chest. "Loser. Same as your old man."

Sammy raised his fists. If Gus hadn't grabbed him, he would have pummeled Carson's smirking face. "Let go so I can kill him," Sammy hissed.

"I don't think so, dude," Gus said. "So not worth it."

"That's right, amigo. So not worth it," Carson said. "You touch me and your dad is fired."

"Is there a *problem* here?" It was Coach Harris.

Sammy shook off Gus and lowered his fists.

Carson gave Coach a crooked smile. "No problem, Coach. Just a dull, wooden discussion." He turned and headed for the dugout.

Coach eyed Sammy. "We're going to Austin, Sammy. Get that into your head. If you don't want to participate, I'll give you a pass this tournament. Let me know by Monday so I can change the roster." He stormed off.

Once Coach was gone, Gus said, "Holy freakin' smokes, Batman. What was that all about?"

"Nothing. Just that I suck and Coach doesn't want me on the team."

"Uh . . . that's not how I heard it."

Sammy shrugged. "Maybe I *shouldn't* play in Austin. I'm not helping the team."

"Our once happy family is so riled. Shall we retire to the locker room and lead a verse of 'Kumbayah'?"

Sammy rolled his eyes. "Let's just get out of here."

As they walked toward the dugout, Gus said, "If a camp song won't calm you down, I have another solution. . . ."

"Gus—"

"A date tomorrow with a lovely young lady who very much wants to meet you."

"I really don't think—"

"You already agreed, dude! And you may change your mind when you hear where we're going." He grinned.

Sammy took a deep breath. "Where?"

Gus paused dramatically. "AT&T Park."

Sammy dropped his jaw. "As in San Francisco?"

"Giants versus Cubs. Via Dad's Gulfstream."

"Are you kidding me?"

"Of course not. I'm always serious about my entertainment."

"Gus, I don't know."

"Dude. Did you see yourself today? I'd say you're due for some major relaxation."

Sammy closed his eyes. His entire body ached with stress. He probably wouldn't be playing in next weekend's tournament anyway, so what was he in training for?

"Okay. Fine."

# CHAPTER 6

Sammy had never before flown in a Gulfstream. The leather seats were big and cushy—the kind you'd find in an expensive house's living room. He used to connect the smell of leather with baseball gloves. But between the seats in Gus's BMW and this jet, Sammy was beginning to link the scent with wealth. It made him physically hungry, like he had a gnawing pit in his stomach that needed filling.

Sammy closed his eyes and rubbed his hands over the seat's buttery surface. He wanted this, for himself and for his family. Sometimes it seemed so close to reality. But when he was playing badly, like this past week, the dream fizzled. That scared him.

"Yo, space cadet!"

Sammy opened his eyes. Gus stood above him, gripping four frosty cans of soda.

"Thanks," Sammy said, grabbing one.

"*De nada.*" Gus handed the girls their drinks before plopping into his seat. The four chairs swiveled and formed a kind of circle. So far, when Gus wasn't jabbering away, Olivia and Kelsey had been whispering to each other.

Kelsey looked over at Sammy and gave him a shy smile before opening her can. She *was* attractive—long brown hair, deep brown eyes, and smooth, tan skin. No matter what Gus said, Sammy wasn't a monk. He'd dated before, but nothing steady. His baseball career interfered with going out, and that's the way he wanted it. Anyway, once a girl realized that conversations with Sammy meant either talking about baseball or long periods of silence, she lost interest.

Sammy would think about a serious relationship later, when he had more time. Maybe when he was in the big leagues. At the moment, he just wanted to relax and not think about the Roadrunners, or wooden bats, or Carson Jamison's breath in his face.

"This is my first big-league game," Kelsey said.

"No way!" Gus said. "I've lost count. That's why Pop got me into Little League. I kept begging him to take me to games all over the country, and he figured playing would be cheaper. He was right."

Kelsey said, "What about you, Sammy? How many games have you been to?"

"Me?" Sammy gripped his can and it crunched. "Uh, well . . ."

"Oh, dude," Gus said. "Don't tell me this is your first too."

Sammy sighed. "Second. My uncle drove me to my only MLB game when I was five, in LA. One of the best days of my life."

"Yeah, that's one of the big drawbacks of living in Vegas," Gus said. "No pro ball."

Gus talked about the latest rumors of which professional sports teams might move to Southern Nevada, and Sammy was relieved for the subject switch. He didn't want to explain that he'd only been to one pro game because his family didn't have enough money to go anywhere. Kelsey glanced over at Sammy with a look that was part sympathy and all warmth. Sammy squirmed. Her smile put a crazy flutter his stomach. He didn't like it.

Sammy had played in some pretty big stadiums, but nothing close to the forty-thousand-seat AT&T Park. He loved the noise of the crowd, the smell of the beer and hotdogs, and the lame but perky music. It reminded him of being a five-year-old at Dodger Stadium. It had taken Sammy only one inning to understand why his dad had wanted to play ball so badly. And it put Sammy on the same course—he wanted to be one of those guys in uniform down on the field.

Knowing Gus's dad, Sammy shouldn't have been surprised when they climbed down the stadium steps instead of up them. Even so, he sucked in a breath when they scooted into their seats three rows behind home plate. Sammy could actually feel his heart beating.

"This is pretty exciting, isn't it?" Kelsey said as they waited for the game to start.

"Yeah, it is."

"You'll be able to see every pitch and swing from here."

He looked at her, surprised. It was exactly what he was thinking. "Yeah. I've never been this close to big-league action before."

She tilted her bag of popcorn toward him. He hesitated before taking a handful.

"By the way, I *like* sports. I'm a center forward on the soccer team at the high school," she said. "And I like baseball, so I'll be watching the game."

Sammy wasn't sure what she meant, so he just muttered, "Okay."

She smiled. "That means we don't need to make conversation. You know, we can just focus on the game."

Between what she'd said and her sweet smile, the dangerous flutter was back in Sammy's stomach. He cleared his throat and repeated, "Okay," before shoving the popcorn in his mouth. He was such an idiot.

As it happened, Sammy talked a lot to Kelsey during the game. She had some basic understanding of baseball and asked interesting questions. One question Sammy didn't have an answer for was why bats were breaking. By the fifth inning, one bat had split in two, the end shooting off into the infield. Another had fractured, but it stayed in one piece.

In the top of the sixth, after a Cubbie hit a double, Kelsey said, "I really like that sound the wooden bat makes. My little brother plays Little League, and the ping from those metal bats just isn't the same. It doesn't sound real."

Sammy had never thought about it like that. But once the thought was in his head, he couldn't get rid of it. *It doesn't sound real.* It was true. Big leaguers would never use aluminum bats. Anything other than wood *wasn't* real.

And then it dawned on Sammy: he *had* to get used to hitting with wooden bats. If his goal was to be a big-league player, then he had no choice. Eventually, he'd have to make the switch. So why wait? Wouldn't using wood now put him ahead of other elite players who put it off?

The Austin tournament was an opportunity to start practicing with wood. And he had a lot to learn.

For the rest of the game, Sammy studied every batter, especially the power hitters. He watched their stances, their swings, their grips. He tracked pitches as they came to the plate, getting a sense of how batters timed their swings. He imagined Wash sitting next to him, giving him pointers.

. . .

On the flight home, Sammy and Kelsey swiveled their seats toward the windows. It was getting dark outside, but even the view of a gray sky was better than watching Gus and Olivia making out in one of the seats across the aisle. Kelsey's eyes were closed, and Sammy wondered if she was sleeping. It had been a long day.

He probably shouldn't have stared, but he liked looking at her. He liked the way her hair curled around her face. He wondered what her lips would feel like against his. Sammy took a deep breath and gazed back out the window. *NO GIRLS! You do not have time for a relationship, Samuel Perez.* He forced his mind back to baseball, remembering what he'd learned at the Giants game. He imagined putting it all together when he got home.

"You look intense," Kelsey said. "You're squinting."

"Yeah. I'm, uh, taking some imaginary swings."

"Cool. You'll get it."

He laughed at her confidence. "You think so?"

"Sure. You seem pretty focused. Like you don't give up easily." She paused and smiled. "I had a really nice time today."

"I did too." The words were out of his mouth before he had a chance to stop them. He didn't want her getting the wrong idea. They wouldn't be going out again. They didn't have a future together.

Kelsey faced the window and closed her eyes.

The flutter in Sammy's stomach was back. He forced himself to smell the leather seat. He brushed his hand over its buttery surface. *This will be mine. This will be my family's.* He liked being hungry, but only for the right things and for the right reasons.

# CHAPTER 7

The idea of using a computer during the summer reminded Sammy too much of school and homework. He typically didn't even update his Facebook page until the fall. But after deciding yesterday at the Giants game that he'd start taking wooden bats seriously, he wanted to learn everything he could about them. So he sat cross-legged on his bed early Sunday morning and opened his laptop.

"Sammy," Thomás mumbled from his bed on the other side of their bedroom. "Is it time to get up?"

"No, T-Rex. Go back to sleep."

Sammy quietly clicked the keyboard and went online. Right away, he found several articles on the differences between composite and wooden bats. He opened a link. The article explained that modern players grow up using aluminum bats, so they look for the same light weight and fast speed when they turn pro. "I totally get *that*," Sammy whispered. He scrolled down the page.

He read that old-style bats used to weigh thirty-six to thirty-eight ounces. In order to make them lighter and faster, but still have a big sweet spot, bat makers started carving the handles thinner and the barrels bigger. Today's wooden bats weigh thirty-two to thirty-four ounces. "'But these changes mean they're much more apt to break,'" Sammy read aloud. It made sense.

Thomás groaned and pulled the blanket over his head.

Sammy clicked on another link. This article said that for a hundred years, bats were only made with wood from the ash tree. Now, about half of all bats are made with maple. The trend started in 2001 when Barry Bonds used maple bats during his big home-run streak. "'The grains in the ash make it flex at the handle, but maple breaks cleanly,'" Sammy whispered. In his mind, he pictured the end of the bat just missing Trip's neck at Friday's practice. And the piece flying into the infield at the Giants game. He bet that both of those bats were made of maple. And the bat that broke but didn't come apart was probably made of ash.

Sammy kept reading. He wasn't surprised to learn that the most expensive pro bats are the thinnest and lightest, and made of maple instead of ash. Of course Carson's dad would buy the most expensive bats out there. He wondered if Mr. Jamison also knew the bats he'd donated could be the most dangerous. Coach and Wash would certainly know. But still, the thought of maple bats splintering into pieces made Sammy nervous. He closed his computer and got dressed.

. . .

After downing a bowl of cereal, Sammy grabbed the wooden bats he'd left in the garage. His dad had fit a small swing set into the backyard, but otherwise Sammy's batting cage took up the whole space. Yet another sacrifice his family made for his baseball career.

He started working off the tee. At first he made good contact. Really good. He blasted the ball with a satisfying crack, certain he was hitting for extra bases. But when he switched to the machine, he either whiffed or tipped. He was too slow on the ball, just like Wash said.

Sammy imagined the pro batters in yesterday's game. He started experimenting, first by opening his stance so he could see the ball better. It helped a little, but then he felt off-balance. To gain more control, he choked up on the bat. That helped him make more contact but lost him power. So he went back to his regular stance, but stepped deep into the box to give himself a little more time to watch the ball. But then he got ahead of the pitch. He could practically hear Wash saying, "You're overthinking it."

"Duh, I know!" Sammy muttered at his imaginary coach. His stomach knotted. His scalp got hot and tight, like his batting helmet had shrunk two sizes. Why was this so difficult?

Eyeing the aluminum bat he kept in the cage, Sammy exchanged it for the wood and instantly felt like he was home. He set the pitching machine at its fastest setting and slammed ball after ball high into the net. But with every satisfying *ping*, he could feel his major-league career sliding down the tubes.

His dad wandered into the backyard as Sammy picked up balls to refill the machine. He was wearing his chauffeur's uniform and holding a mug of coffee. "How's it working?" he asked.

"If you mean the pitching machine, it's working fine."

His dad took a sip of coffee. "Mrs. Martinez called. Said you should know better than to use your batting cage at eight o'clock on a Sunday morning."

"Sorry."

His dad shrugged, smiling. "That's what I told her. And that you wouldn't do it again." He dumped the rest of his coffee onto the grass. "I was watching you from the kitchen window. Your timing is off."

"Yeah, Dad, I *know* my timing is off. I'm making adjustments."

Then, slowly, like he was carefully choosing his words, his dad said, "If you were stronger, you know, especially arm strength . . . you could get the bat off your shoulder quicker."

Sammy loaded the balls into the machine. His dad wasn't talking about getting stronger from weight training or from drinking protein shakes. He was talking about PEDs again.

Sammy's stomach clenched like it always did when he thought about using steroids. At the start of every season, Coach Harris gave the Runners his *Evils of PEDs* lecture. There were long-term health effects, like liver, heart, and reproductive damage. Not to mention a chance of getting caught and banned from baseball. Coach said there was no safe dosage, no matter what anyone said.

But Sammy understood where his dad was coming from. Big leaguers and other top athletes used PEDs all the time. Bulking up gave them an edge. For Sammy, that edge could mean the difference between being a top draft pick and not being drafted at all.

In any event, it was a topic on which Sammy didn't want to linger. "So you're working today?"

"Overtime. Some friends of Jamison's are in town. He said he'd let them use his limo if I was willing to drive them on my day off."

"Are you kidding me? Dad, you work all the time!"

He shrugged. "There's only one supplier for those pitching machine parts. They screw you on the price."

Sammy looped his fingers through the batting-cage netting and stared at his dad. "I should be working. I should have a job like everyone else in this family."

"You have a job, son. Hitting is your job. See you tonight." He walked toward the house.

Sammy closed his eyes and squeezed his fingers around the net. "Dad. Wait."

He turned.

"That sports doc. I think . . . Can you set an appointment for me?"

His dad nodded and walked into the house.

# CHAPTER 8

Monday morning, with Wash watching, Sammy took some swings off a batting tee. Wash shook his head, sucking air through his teeth. Not a good sign.

"What did you do to yourself over the weekend?" Wash asked. "You look like a five-year-old whiffing a T-ball."

Sammy groaned. He knew Wash was mostly teasing, but the comment just added to his frustration. "I was trying to fix it."

"Well, you made it worse. The tournament is in four days. Thursday is travel. That leaves today, Tuesday, and Wednesday to get your swing in shape."

Sammy pounded the end of his bat into the dirt. "I don't think that's possible. I should've told Coach I wouldn't go."

"The problem is not the problem. The problem is your attitude about the problem."

Wash liked using mottoes to make a point. Still pounding the bat, Sammy watched the dust billowing up and landing on his cleats. "So you're telling me I have an attitude problem."

"Well . . . don't you?"

Sammy raised his eyes. Coming from one of his teammates, those words would have earned a shove, maybe a punch. But he respected Wash too much. "So, what, I should start sleeping with my bat? Write it love poetry?"

Wash grinned. "Couldn't hurt. Although it might make more sense to return to basics."

"Basics. Great," Sammy mumbled.

"*Attitude*, Sammy."

He pasted a smile on his face. "Basics! Great!"

"Much better." Wash hesitated. "I'm going to talk to Coach. Just . . . stay put." He trotted to the dugout.

Ten minutes later Wash was back, carrying several bats and donut weights. Somehow he'd talked Coach into letting Sammy work only on batting before they flew to Austin. It was a surprising move, since Coach liked his players to work as a team this close to big games.

"You guys must be pretty worried about my problem," Sammy said.

"Well . . . in a word, yes. You're one of the team's best hitters, Sammy. *The* best hitter when you're hot."

What Wash didn't say, what he didn't *have* to say, was that without Sammy's big bat, the Runners were more likely to lose. When the team lost, they went down in the standings, which hurt everyone—coaches and players. They got fewer good invites. And when it came to tournaments, losing meant playing in fewer big games, which meant fewer chances to impress scouts.

"Is this a single- or double-elimination tournament?" Sammy wondered aloud.

"Single. Twenty top-tier teams."

"So there's no losers' bracket?"

"No. There's a three-game guarantee, but—"

"But scouts won't be watching meaningless games."

Wash shrugged. "Maybe. Not as likely."

Sammy's stomach rolled. He took a deep breath, feeling a huge opportunity slipping away. If they lost their first game, goodbye scouts. Goodbye one more chance to go pro. "So, help me, Wash. What do I need to do?"

Wash slapped Sammy's back. "First, try to relax. You've got big shoulders, but the entire team isn't sitting up there."

Sammy didn't dare tell Wash he was more worried about himself than the team.

"Second," Wash said, "we won't throw the baby out with the bathwater. You're a good hitter with a nice swing, so we want to keep most of what you've got. The goal is to get you swinging faster, but to still have power and control. Less is more."

To reach Wash's goal, Sammy ended up with the lightest bat—thirty-two ounces. He also choked another half inch, and he stood slightly deeper and more open in the box. They were small adjustments, but they gave Sammy a split second longer to watch the ball before committing.

"Now all you need is practice," Wash said, once he was satisfied with Sammy's progress. "Lots and lots of practice."

. . .

Sammy did practice, at home as well as at the park. By Wednesday, he was hitting a variety of pitches with wood. He felt better, but not confident. One of Wash's sayings ran through Sammy's head: *If you think you can, you can. If you think you can't, you're right.*

Two more bats broke apart during the Runners' practice games that week. The broken ends didn't hurt anyone, and Sammy sure hoped it stayed that way.

# CHAPTER *9*

*T*he Roadrunners flew into Austin on
Thursday afternoon. Twenty teams
was a big tournament. And Sammy couldn't
believe how many players swarmed the lobby
of the Austin Hyatt, where Coach had booked
them. Some of these guys they'd met before,
like the Bulldogs from Reno and the El Paso
Gila Monsters. Others were new competition.

Like the Runners, some teams were
switching to wooden bats just for this

tournament. Others were in leagues that only used wood. The Roadrunners hadn't played any wooden-league teams before, so they were a big question mark. Hopefully Wash had done his homework.

After they'd settled into their rooms, The Runners met with Coach Harris in one of the hotel's small conference rooms. Wash and Nellie handed out the tournament schedule. Coach announced, "The park is four blocks from the hotel, so we'll be walking. There are two fields. Pay attention to where you're supposed to be. I want you stretching and throwing the ball thirty minutes before game time. First game is Friday at 10:30. Next is 3:00. The semifinal is Saturday at 3:00, and the final is Sunday at 1:30. Any questions about the schedule?"

"Um . . . that's if we win all our games, Coach," Danny said. "What if we lose?"

"That's not gonna happen." Coach glared at Danny, then swiveled his head and met everyone's eyes. "You all know how to win. Using wooden bats is no excuse." Coach held his gaze on Sammy, who squirmed and looked down at the schedule in his hands. He sensed other players looking at him too.

"Coach," Carson said, "can I just remind everyone we're doing this for TJ?"

Sammy knew Carson's statement was mostly directed at him.

"That's right," Coach said. "Let's win this tournament for TJ!"

"TJ!" a few of the players yelled.

Sammy joined in the cheer. He was annoyed at Carson, but he also felt like a jerk. He liked TJ. And he'd been so wrapped up with his own hitting problems that he'd completely forgotten about TJ's career-ending injury. The same injury might have happened with a wooden bat, like his dad had said. But Sammy wasn't so sure.

Wash ended the meeting with a rundown of the San Jose Mustangs, their first opponent.

. . .

As Sammy and Gus strolled through the lobby on their way to the elevator, they overheard bits of excited conversation:

"Not *just* MLB scouts, man. Regional supervisors and cross-checkers and scouting directors. They're all here . . . !"

". . . Big 12, PAC 10, SEC . . ."

"This is as good as a national showcase . . ."

Sammy walked faster, wanting to clamp his hands over his ears.

"Dude, hold up!" Gus trotted to catch up. "Do you hafta pee or something?"

"No. I'm just . . . I think this whole tournament is a waste."

"You better hope not. Did you hear all of that chatter? If it's true, we may not go to a better tournament all season. This may be your big break, dude!" He grinned and punched Sammy's arm.

Sammy's stomach churned. The scouts would be witnessing a power hitter who couldn't hit. *Sammy fail.* "I need to go to our room and chill."

"Don't chill too long. I'm in the mood for some Tex-Mex. There's a sizzling steak fajita out there with my name on it."

The thought of food made Sammy want to hurl.

# CHAPTER 10

Sammy stepped onto the field at 9:45 A.M. He hadn't slept much and felt like a zombie. The Roadrunners had never met the guys they were facing. According to Wash, the San Jose Mustangs were a talented team that usually used aluminum bats, just like the Runners. The Mustangs didn't have a lot of pitching depth, but the hurler they were playing this morning was their best. Excellent speed and control, and he worked well inside. Just Sammy's luck.

Other than Nellie, the Runners' team captain, Sammy was the first player to arrive at the field. He'd left Gus in the hotel's dining room, chowing down on his tenth toaster waffle. The place swarmed with yelling, nerve-amped ballplayers. Sammy ate a yogurt and a couple of hardboiled eggs and split for the field.

Sitting and stretching into a toe-touch, Sammy glanced into the stands. A few people trickled in. Most were fans and parents, which Sammy could tell by their shorts and cameras and armfuls of snacks. He recognized Nellie's mom and dad, who went to almost every game. They waved at Sammy. He waved back. They chatted with their son over the third-baseline fence. Sammy's family only went to games the Runners played near Vegas. Airfare was too expensive. He couldn't remember the last time his dad had seen him play. But that would change once Sammy got his first MLB contract. He'd fly his family everywhere. That was, *if* he got his first contract.

Leaning back into a twisting stretch, Sammy scanned the stands for scouts. They were usually middle-aged men wearing long pants, even on hot days like this. And they always sat alone, close to the field or higher up in the stands, depending on whom they were watching. Scouts studied players with small, high-powered binoculars. But the biggest giveaway was the clipboard or notebook. While other spectators clapped and cheered after a big play, scouts lowered their heads and jotted notes.

Sammy didn't see anyone who fit that description . . . yet. But if the rumors were true, they'd be here.

The excitement level shot up as more players from both teams began arriving. Sammy momentarily forgot about the people in the stands and focused on his job. The Runners were the home team, which meant the Mustangs were batting first. That was fine with Sammy. The longer he put off his first at bat, the better. That thought surprised and also depressed him. The batter's box used to be his favorite place in the world. He punched his fist into his glove and forced himself to mutter some chatter at the Mustangs' first batter.

Fumio Kimura was pitching for the Roadrunners. His stuff was good. The top of the first inning quickly ended with a grounder to Trip at shortstop, a foul pop-up to Nellie at third, and a comebacker to Fumio.

As always, Darius led off the batting order for the Runners. His hitting was a little inconsistent, but he had amazing speed. Sammy usually batted cleanup, but for this game Coach had him batting seventh. It was embarrassing and made Sammy angry, but he was angry with himself—it wasn't Coach's fault Sammy wasn't hitting.

The Runners' first inning at bat was uneventful. After two quick outs, Nellie got on base with a hard line drive to right, which at least showed that the Mustangs' pitcher could be hit. But the pitcher got it together and struck out Trip for the last out of the inning.

Sammy would be batting third next inning. He took a deep breath and trotted to right field.

"Sammy, check it out!" Danny called from center. "Cave man!" He pointed his glove toward the infield.

Lumbering up to the plate was the Mustangs' huge left fielder—their cleanup batter. He was well over six feet tall, with tree-trunk arms. Did he work out a lot, Sammy wondered, or was he doing something artificial to bulk up? Sammy wondered if his dad had set up his appointment with the sports doc yet. Would he develop tree-trunk arms too?

Tree Trunk had a good eye and really worked Fumio, fouling off or looking at everything Fumio sent him. Sammy lost count of the number of pitches. Then, on a three-and-two count, Fumio must have taken something off his fastball. There was a tremendous *CRACK*, and Sammy watched a towering drive soar toward center field. Danny raced back for it, but Sammy knew it was just to show off his hustling skills for the scouts. The ball easily shot over the fence with room to spare.

Sammy peered into the stands as fans cheered. He saw at least three middle-aged men with their heads lowered. A few more guys had their expensive binoculars trained on the home run hitter prancing around the bases like he owned the diamond.

Sammy pressed his hands on his hips and pounded his cleats into the grass. He felt a mixture of envy and admiration. The kid had an artificial edge. He must. But it didn't matter a bit to the scouts. All they saw was a seventeen-year-old slugger who could whack a baseball with a wooden bat over the center field fence. Every MLB team wanted that kind of talent on its roster. Sammy again wondered if his dad had set the appointment to see the sports doctor.

Nick Cosimo, the Runners' catcher, chatted with Fumio on the mound. That seemed to settle him down, and Fumio got the next three batters out in order. The score was one-zip.

When Sammy came up to bat in the bottom of the second, the image of Tree Trunk's towering line drive replayed in his head. In the infield, the Runners' second baseman, Danny, took a short lead off second. He'd reached first on a single, then raced to second after Zack laid down a perfect sacrifice bunt. There was one out.

From the coach's box, Wash held his fist in front of his chest and stuck out his little finger. It was the signal to sacrifice. That meant they expected Nick, who was batting after Sammy, to get Danny home, not Sammy.

"Take it easy," Wash chattered at Sammy, clapping his hands.

Sammy's cheeks burned. Maybe he wasn't bulked up, but he could hit. Darn it, he was a power hitter! He'd proven himself time and again, without PEDs. Wood or aluminum, a bat was a bat. A slugger was a slugger!

He stepped into the box and took his stance. The Mustangs' pitcher shook off his catcher's first sign, and then he nodded. His quick throw curved far inside, and Sammy jumped back to get out of the way.

He heard Wash clapping and chanting, "Easy, Sammy. Easy easy."

The next pitch was an inside fastball but without much speed. Sammy was supposed to sacrifice. That meant a slow grounder to first, a bunt, or a long fly ball.

In a split second, Sammy thought, *I'm not taking it easy!* He swung and he swung hard. The awkward jerk of the bat and the dead *clunk* told Sammy he'd hit the ball, but not solidly. He sprinted down the baseline while the ball hung in the air and eventually dropped between the charging outfielder and the backpedaling second baseman. A blooper base hit. Danny advanced to third and Sammy was safe at first.

Some cheers sprang out of the dugout. Sammy shook his head. "Crap." He didn't want to look at Wash. He'd moved Danny over to third, but now they were set up for a double play.

"What were you thinking, Sammy?" Wash asked from the coach's box.

Sammy finally glanced at him. "Sorry, Wash. I thought I could hit for extra bases."

"Listen to me next time, okay?"

Sammy nodded, wanting to sink into the ground.

"On your toes, now," Wash said.

Sammy forced himself to get his head back in the game. Nick was at the plate. Sammy took a long lead off first, as far as he dared stretch it. The pitcher eyed Sammy once. Twice. He threw to first, and Sammy just got back in time. Sammy would never forgive himself if he got tagged leaning, but he was riled. He wanted to make up for his stupid at bat by stealing second. Glancing at Wash, Sammy raised an eyebrow. Wash hesitated, but then nodded with a frown.

Sammy understood Wash's mixed message. *Steal if you can, but be smart about it.* Sammy stepped off of first with a slightly shorter lead than before. The pitcher eyed him a few times, then pitched to Nick, who swung and missed. Unlike Sammy, the Runners' catcher hadn't had difficulty making the switch to wood. He tended to make contact off the end of his bat instead of the lower barrel, where wood and aluminum weren't shaped all that differently.

Determined to steal on the next pitch, Sammy extended his lead. The second the pitcher released the ball, Sammy committed, tearing down the base path. Nick must have really liked the pitch, because he swung and made contact. But instead of a solid hit, he slapped a slow grounder to third. Out of the corner of his eye, Sammy saw the third baseman scoop up the ball, hold Zack on, and throw to second. Sammy had a good jump and was already in a straight-leg slide. He skimmed over second base, hooking his top leg under the second baseman's foot.

"Safe!" the second-base umpire yelled.

Sammy scrambled to his feet and watched the second baseman throw off-balance to first. The errant ball sailed past the first baseman's outstretched glove and into foul territory. Danny scored. And Sammy advanced to third on the broken-up double play. There was still just one out.

Pressing his hands on his knees, Sammy sucked in air. The guys in the dugout were cheering and high-fiving Danny. A part of Sammy's brain knew he'd made a good play. But in the long run, it was meaningless. Lots of guys were fast. Lots of guys could break up double plays.

*You're a power hitter,* Sammy heard his dad saying. *It's what you do.*

Sammy was just glad his dad wasn't here to watch him fall short of both of their expectations. He didn't dare look in the stands to see the scouts *not* watching him.

# CHAPTER 11

While standing at third base, Sammy had a chance to cool down and think. Following a coach's orders was important. It meant you were a team player, easy to work with. Attitude was included in scouting reports. Given a choice between players of equal skill, an MLB team would always draft a swell guy like Nellie ahead of a loner and hothead like Sammy.

The second inning ended with Fumio

striking out, followed by Darius hitting a line drive right into the shortstop's glove.

As Sammy trotted into the dugout, Gus fist-bumped him. "Good breakup, dude. Too bad we left you out there."

Sammy shrugged.

"Nice sliding," Coach Harris said. "But next time do what Wash tells you. This is a team sport, not the Sammy Perez sport."

"I know, Coach." Sammy hunted out Wash, who was jotting notes on the lineup sheet. "I'm sorry," Sammy said. "I should have taken your signal."

Wash looked up from his clipboard and slowly nodded. "You're still not comfortable up there. So stop swinging at early pitches. Get a feel for what's coming over the plate. Patience is the companion of wisdom, Sammy."

He sighed at yet another one of Wash's proverbs. "Got it." Grabbing his glove, he trotted into right field.

Patience wasn't one of Sammy's strengths, no matter how wise Wash thought it made him. With aluminum, nine times out of ten the coaches gave him his freedom and let him swing away. But with wood, it was different. For the rest of the game, Sammy did what Wash and Coach Harris wanted. In three more at bats, Sammy watched the pitches. He struck out twice and popped up on a three-and-two count. Every patient at bat drove him crazy. He did feel uncomfortable. And anxious. And even worse, he lacked confidence. It didn't take one of Wash's old sayings for Sammy to know that the worse he felt, the worse he played.

Despite his individual struggles, the Roadrunners squeaked out a four-to-three win, due mainly to Fumio's five-hit, complete game. The Mustangs' pitcher self-destructed in the sixth, when both Gus and Trip singled and Nellie slammed a home run. Except for Fumio, Sammy was the only Runner without a solid hit, since he didn't count the blooper.

In the locker room, Fumio and Nellie soaked up the praise. Sammy could sense everyone's relief. Since they had won, they weren't facing a meaningless loser's game. And except for him, none of the guys had embarrassed themselves in front of the scouts, who would still be watching tomorrow. Sammy sat in the corner, taking off his shoes and packing his bag.

"You guys did okay," Coach announced. "Good hitting from most of you. We need to make 'em all count next time. Too many stranded base runners.

"I know some of you are still uncomfortable with the changed lineup," he continued, glancing over at Sammy. "But we're going to keep it as is for the next game." What he didn't have to say was that the batting lineup would stay that way until Sammy started hitting again. "Be at Field A at 2:15."

Gus and Sammy walked together to the hotel to grab some lunch. "Sorry about the batting situation, dude," Gus said. "Do you wanna talk about it?"

"No."

"Didn't think so." Gus's iPhone buzzed, and a grin spread across his face as he read the text message. Looking up, Gus cleared his throat. "Um, I don't want to add to your stress, but that was from Olivia. I'm afraid Kelsey likes you."

Only Gus would know that a girl liking Sammy would stress him out. And it did. Sammy's stomach got that uncomfortable, crazy flutter. "That's too bad."

"Yeah, that's what I'm going to text her back: *Lo siento.* Kelsey better not count on getting a phone call from you for like the next three years."

Sammy shoved his hands in his pockets. He imagined Kelsey's silky brown hair curving around her beautiful face. When he'd talked to her at the Giants game, she was actually interested in what he had to say. But, by the time Sammy went pro, where would Kelsey be? Not waiting for him.

He could feel Gus staring. "What are you looking at?"

Gus gasped dramatically. "Dude, you really like her, don't you?"

Sammy didn't dare say anything.

"You *really, really* like her. . . ." A grin spread across Gus's face. Sammy wanted to smack him.

"Cool it! I can't do a relationship now. I have to focus."

Gus shrugged. "Whatever. It's your life, dude. Your focused, miserable life."

"Hey!" Sammy shoved Gus's arm. "I'm *not* miserable."

"Oh yeah, I forgot. You enjoy a full range of life experiences. And you laugh. All the time."

Sammy glared at Gus, who mumbled innocently, "What?"

. . .

As Sammy stretched on the field for their three o'clock game, he didn't look in the stands for scouts. It was too depressing. Nellie sank onto the grass near him and did some toe touches. After stretching quietly for a minute, Nellie said, "There's been some talk."

Sammy stopped stretching and glanced over at Nellie.

"A few of the guys think you're screwing up on purpose."

"What?" Sammy sat up straight.

"They think you're so angry about going to this wooden tournament that you're not trying."

"That's not true!"

"That's what I told them. I think you're in a real slump. The thing is, you've got the skills to get drafted. Or at least to play Division 1. But when you aren't hitting, it keeps us from winning games, which hurts the other guys trying to get to the next level. Like for Darius and Zack, baseball scholarships are everything. They can't afford college without them."

"I am trying," Sammy hissed.

"I know. Just think about what I said. Try harder or something. You're a member of the Roadrunners, remember. We're a team." Nellie got to his feet and trotted over to the third baseline, where he talked to his parents, who were again sitting in the front row.

Sammy frowned, clenching his jaw. He couldn't magically produce hits, just because

Darius and Zack needed college scholarships. And by following Wash's instructions during his last three at bats, hadn't he proved in the last game he was a *team player*? What the hell did they expect him to do?

# CHAPTER *12*

For their second game, the Runners faced the Austin Athletics, an all-wood team playing in their hometown. Local players always attracted lots of fans, and the stands were packed. This time the Runners were the away team and up at bat first. Unless the top of the order was very productive, Sammy wouldn't be coming to the plate this inning. Like in the last game, that was fine with him.

Darius was at the plate, leading off for the Runners, and Gus was on deck. As Sammy leaned back against the bench, he realized no one was sitting near him. Were they afraid his slump was contagious? Or was it like Nellie had said, and they were pissed because they thought he was faking it?

There was a *crack-crunch* as Darius connected with a fastball—a broken bat. Sammy jumped to his feet and yelled, "Heads up!" as the end of the bat flew into the Athletics' dugout. But it happened so fast that the shard had already smashed against the dugout wall. Luckily, no one was hit.

Sammy took a relieved breath. Why did Mr. Jamison have to go with maple bats?

. . .

According to Wash, the Athletics' pitcher was a control freak with a nasty curve and a good change-up. Through six innings, the guy was hot and really worked the plate. He held the Runners to three unproductive hits. The

Athletics led the game, having scored two runs off Runners pitcher Kurt Kincaid in the third.

In the dugout before the top of the seventh, Coach said, "He's thrown seventy-two pitches. Make him work for an out. Get him tired. But if you see something you like, go for it."

Nellie went to the plate and hit into a ground out to shortstop. Trip then hit a long drive into left that almost dropped, but the fielder made a miraculous shoe-string grab. When Danny came up, he hit his second pitch off the first baseman's glove for a single. Then Zack slapped his first pitch past the third baseman. And just like that, men on first and on second with two outs.

Sammy was up.

The Athletics' catcher trotted to the mound as Sammy walked to the plate. Was the pitcher really losing it, Sammy wondered? He rolled his shoulders and loosely swung the bat. His first two at bats had been busts: a pop-up and then a ground out. Thankfully, no one was on base either time.

He glanced over at Wash, but with two outs and two men on, he only had two choices: hit or walk. Clapping his hands, Wash called, "Patience, Sammy. See the ball."

From the dugout came, "Slug it, Sammy!" "Go for it!" "Home run!" "You can do it, man!"

Sammy took a deep breath. He used to love the dugout chatter. The pressure pumped him up and got him focused. If he were using his aluminum bat, he'd get a hit and a couple of ribbies, no problem. But with this wooden stick? He teammates wanted him to get them ahead with a single swing. Wash still wanted him to be patient. Sammy didn't know what to do.

The catcher trotted back behind the plate. Sammy stepped into the box. The pitcher squinted at the signals, his lips pressed together in a thin line and his jaw tight. He might have been tiring, Sammy thought, but he was focused. He probably still had some good pitches left.

Sammy raised his bat over his shoulder, regripping the handle. The pitcher wound and extended. Sammy watched the release point and tracked the ball. It was curving inside, a little high. It was Sammy's pitch. Rather, it used to be his pitch. It wasn't his pitch with wood, and he forced himself to hold up. The ump called ball one. Sammy let out the breath he'd been holding.

Closing up to the plate, Sammy shrunk his strike zone by a couple of inches. Expecting a fastball, he instead got another curve, this time in the strike zone. It was lower than Sammy liked, but he decided it was better to make contact than to watch a strike. He swung and fouled to the left.

The next pitch was an inside fastball that sunk low for ball two.

"Come on, Sammy!" he heard from the dugout.

Sammy shook his head, more for himself than for whoever had yelled. He wanted to slug a home run more than anything. But if he popped up or grounded out, his teammates would kill him. Shoot, he'd want to kill himself. He decided to wait for the right pitch,

and if it didn't come . . . so be it. The count
reached three and two and stayed that way
for the next five pitches, which were all in
the strike zone. Sammy connected with all of
them for fouls.

"Loser! Hit it already!" Carson yelled.

Sammy hardly heard the taunt. He was in
a zone, one completely new to him. He'd never
been a finesse hitter, because he hadn't had
to be. But now he was truly seeing each and
every pitch. Since none of them were *his* pitch,
he swatted them away like flies.

The pitcher stepped off the mound, his head
down. When he returned, Sammy saw that his
eyes drooped a little and the laser-like focus was
gone. He was tiring. After throwing off a couple
of signs from his catcher, the pitcher hurled. It
was a curveball, high and inside, similar to the
first pitch Sammy had seen. It was so close to his
perfect pitch. So close! Sammy started to swing.
But it was too high. He held up.

Ball four.

Sammy trotted to first base. There wasn't
much response from the dugout, other than

Gus's "Good eye, dude!" What could his teammates say? They might have been disappointed that he hadn't slugged a home run, but he'd reached first to load the bases. Based on what Nellie had told him, Sammy wondered how many Roadrunners thought he hadn't hit on purpose.

Wash gave him a small, knowing smile from the coach's box. "Quality at bat, Sammy."

Sammy nodded, but he didn't return Wash's smile. It *was* a quality at bat. He felt a real sense of satisfaction about winning that battle with the pitcher. But the fact remained that he was first and foremost a power hitter. Power hitters hit. They didn't mess around in pitching duels, waiting for the *exact* right pitch.

Carson's taunt should have made Sammy angry, but it was true. He *was* a loser. And if his dad were here, he'd say the same thing.

Nick came to the plate, and Sammy forced his head back into the game. Nick was a solid hitter and had been making good contact this tournament. Maybe Sammy's long at bat had at least worn down the pitcher. Sure enough, a couple of pitches later, Nick hit a change-up over the plate for a double into the right alley. Zack and Danny scored. And with Kurt, the Runners' pitcher, batting next, Coach waved Sammy home. Sammy put on the afterburners and slid under the tag.

The Roadrunners went ahead three to two. Kurt grounded out to end the inning. The Athletics lifted their struggling starter for a pinch hitter in the bottom of the seventh, but neither team got another run. The Runners won, sending the local fans home disappointed.

In the locker room after the game, Coach said, "Another close one. A little more padding would be nice. Our semifinal is tomorrow at three. Don't know yet who we'll be meeting. But it doesn't matter, it will be a hard game." Coach ended his locker-room speech with, "Any questions?"

Nellie raised his hand. "Not a question, but I want to remind everyone about the team dinner tonight. El Tajon, two blocks from the hotel. Six o'clock."

"All right!" Nick yelled. Gus whooped.

In his isolated spot in the corner, Sammy finished changing his shoes and stuffing his bag. Amid the team's happy winning-game talk and laughter, Sammy heard, "Good base running." He looked up. It was Danny.

"Thanks," Sammy said. Although they played in the outfield together, Sammy didn't talk much to the small center fielder. Danny could be a show-off. "Something on your mind?" Sammy asked.

"Um. Yeah," Danny said. "You know there are scouts at this tournament, right?"

"That's what they say. I'm not paying much attention."

"Well, it may not a big deal to you, but there are some reps here for a couple of schools I'm interested in. Just small colleges. They'll probably be at our semifinal tomorrow."

Sammy finished packing his bag and stood. "So?"

"So the better the Runners play, the better we'll look. The better *I'll* look. Especially if we get to the final game."

It hit Sammy that Danny was one of the guys Nellie had talked about—the ones who thought Sammy was faking his hitting slump. "Wait a minute," Sammy protested. "I don't know what you think, but I'm not—"

"You're our best hitter," Danny interrupted. "And . . . well . . . that's all I have to say." He turned and strode off.

Sammy shook his head. Wash was wrong when he said the team wasn't sitting on his shoulders. They were up there, and they weighed a ton.

# CHAPTER *13*

"Come on, dude, you have to eat! It's a team dinner. Everyone's gonna be there."

Sammy lay on his hotel bed with his hands behind his head. "The team hates me. I'll grab something from the vending machines."

"Get up." Gus kicked Sammy's bed. "You're whining. It's *unprofessional.*"

Sammy tossed his pillow at Gus.

"See? Gus laughed. "I know all your *caliente* buttons."

Groaning, Sammy dragged himself off the bed. It was true. He considered whining to be about the most unprofessional thing an athlete could do. And he'd been doing way too much of it lately. "I didn't want a bag of peanuts for dinner anyway."

. . .

The team had a separate room reserved at the restaurant. Sammy grabbed a chair at the long table and Gus sat to his right. As other Runners trickled in, it didn't surprise Sammy that no one took the empty spot to his left. He buried his face in his menu, wanting to disappear. He wished he'd stayed at the hotel.

"Can I sit here?"

Sammy looked up. "TJ?" It took him a second to register that the Roadrunners' former ace pitcher stood next to him. "No. I mean, sure. Have a seat."

As TJ pulled out the chair, Sammy couldn't help staring. There was no outer evidence that TJ's jaw had been broken by that comebacker a year ago. "You look good," Sammy said.

"Thanks. They're still doing some work on my teeth, but otherwise I'm pretty much good as new."

"So . . . what are you doing here?"

"I live in Austin now, with my mom. It's a long story. Nellie got in touch with me, said you guys were in this wooden tournament because of me."

The waitress took their drink orders. When she left, Sammy asked, "Did you see us play today?"

TJ shook his head. "Even watching games on TV freaks me a little. My shrink says I'll have PTSD symptoms for a while."

Sammy felt a wrenching twist in his stomach. Of all the Roadrunners' pitchers, TJ had been his favorite. He was super talented and as serious about the game as Sammy. They had been on the same track—MLB draft.

"Do you miss it?" Sammy asked. "Playing ball, I mean?"

The waitress set down their soft drinks. TJ thoughtfully unwrapped his straw. "It's weird. I thought I would. But then I realized there were these other things I wanted do with my life." His eyes brightened. "I've decided to become an architect. Weird, huh? I've got a college picked out. I actually like school now. My grades are good enough to get an academic scholarship, if you can believe it."

"I can believe it. You don't give up easily." As Sammy drank his soda, he remembered Kelsey saying the same thing about him after the Giants game.

"Hey, it's TJ!" someone shouted. The team suddenly realized their old pitcher sat among them, and they bombarded him with questions.

Sammy was left pondering his conversation with TJ. What if he got injured before his ball career got started? It happened to TJ. It happened to his dad. What if he didn't get drafted? The way this tournament was going, that was a real possibility. Would he end up as a chauffeur for some rich casino director?

Once he started thinking about a future life without baseball, it stuck in his head like a stupid song. That night he woke up sweating, his heart pounding. He had to get drafted so his dad wouldn't have to work anymore. So he could move his family out of that tiny house. So he could pay them back everything they'd sacrificed for him. So he wouldn't have to get some menial job.

He *had* to play pro ball.

# CHAPTER *14*

$A$fternoon games were terrible in a state as hot as Texas. And hanging around waiting for most of the day before the semifinal was brutal on Sammy's already strung-out nerves. He'd never dreaded a game as much as he did this one. There would probably be more scouts in the stands. Teammates like Danny were counting on him to have a big game so they'd all look good and get to the final. And he needed to play well for his own future. Yet Sammy had no more confidence today than he did yesterday, or the day before that, that he could hit solidly with a wooden bat.

As he tied his cleats in the air-conditioned locker room, Sammy envied Gus, who was chatting and joking with Nick. Gus loved baseball, but he loved his life more. If baseball wasn't in his future, he'd enjoy whatever came his way. Of course, having a wealthy family helped take the pressure off. Why did it so often come down to money? Sammy threw his bag into the locker and slammed the door.

Coach stood on one of the benches. "Listen up, everyone!" The locker room quieted. "We're playing the Reno Bulldogs. As you know, we've met these guys before. We're evenly matched. Except unlike our squeakers, the Dogs whaled their opponents in their first two games. That means they've got some confidence. That's okay, we can beat them."

After sharing some bits of information on their pitcher and other players, Wash said, "The batting order has changed." He looked down at his clipboard. "Trip, you're batting fifth. Danny sixth. Zack seventh. Sammy, you're at cleanup. Otherwise, it's the same."

There was a low murmur among the players.

"Play smart, and play hard," Coach Harris said. "Any questions?"

No one answered.

"We're the home team. Get on the field and warm up."

Sammy searched out Wash as the locker room emptied. "What's up with the batting order?"

"You're in your normal position. I thought you'd be happy."

"But Wash, I'm not hitting! Why are you making me cleanup?"

Wash looked Sammy in the eyes. "Maybe Harris and I see something in you that that you don't see in yourself. We didn't make this decision lightly."

As Wash walked out of the locker room, Sammy shook his head in dismay. He quickly grabbed his glove and walked onto the field.

Halfway between home plate and first base, he heard a familiar voice shout, "Sammy!" With a catch in his throat, Sammy saw his dad waving from the front row in the stands. Alexander Jamison sat next to him. Sammy trotted over. "Dad, how—"

"Mr. Jamison wanted to watch Carson pitch. He needed a driver when he got here and knew I'd like to see you play." He shrugged.

Mr. Jamison said, "How are the bats working out, Sammy?" He smirked like he'd donated a million dollars to charity.

Sammy had the sudden urge to slap the fake generosity off that pinched face and tell him the bats were crap. But he knew it wouldn't do any good. "The bats are fine."

His dad whispered, "Lots of scouts here. Some are probably here for you."

"Yeah. Look, I need to get to the outfield."

"Sure. Slam 'em, Sammy!" His dad swung a pretend bat.

Sammy hadn't seen his dad this excited in a long time. But of all the games for him to come to, why did it have to be this one?

The top of the first was uneventful. Carson walked the second batter, but got the side out on a strike, a grounder, and a pop-up. If having his dad in the stands made Carson nervous, he didn't show it. As much as Sammy disliked Carson's snobbery, he was all business on the mound. That's why Coach saved him for big-pressure games.

The Bulldogs' pitcher returned the favor when the Runners came up in the bottom of the first, retiring Darius, Gus, and Nellie in order. Sammy had faced this pitcher before. He had a burning fastball, and when he was hot, he was almost impossible to hit. So far, he was hot.

Even though Carson's speed and control were also working, in the second inning the Bulldogs' big center fielder, a lefty and a pull hitter, made contact with a low fastball. His towering solo home run sailed over the right-alley fence. After the hit, Danny made a motion against his arm, like he was shooting himself with a hypodermic needle. Sammy shook his head at Danny's stupid gesture, hoping no one in the stands had seen it. But Sammy did wonder if the guy was bulked up on PEDs. His big arms and chest reminded Sammy of the tree-trunk batter in yesterday's first game.

After Carson had the side retired, Sammy came to the plate with the score one-zip in the bottom of the second. At least he knew how they'd pitch him—inside, like everyone else had pitched him. Sammy got into his stance and loosely swung his bat. He still disliked the wooden stick, but he was a little more used to it.

Wash clapped his hands from the coach's box. "Relax, Sammy. Be smart. Use your eyes."

Sammy took a deep breath. The pitcher nodded, wound up, and fired an absolute burner. Sammy was jammed and didn't attempt to swing. Strike one.

Sammy had barely raised his bat again, when the pitcher delivered the exact same pitch. The result was the same too. A strike. Sammy shook his head. He could feel his Dad's deepening frown from here. Tapping his bat on the plate, he raised it over his shoulder. He silently repeated Wash's order. *Be smart.* While his emotions told him to slug a home run for his dad, his teammates, and whatever scouts might still be watching, his brain reminded him he was up first. He just needed to get on base. Nothing big, nothing fancy.

The next pitch was another inside burner. If he didn't make contact, he'd be called out on strikes. Sammy timed the pitch and swung. *Plunk.* He hit it down into the dirt, a slow bouncer between the mound and third. The pitcher charged. Sammy had a good jump and sprinted with everything he had. He raced over the bag, unaware he was safe until he turned and saw the ump with his arms still out.

There were a few cheers from the dugout as Sammy walked back to the bag. Since he heard nothing from the front row of the stands, he assumed his dad was disappointed with the wimpy hit. He didn't dare look up there to see that unhappy face.

"Good running," Wash said. "Now read the pitcher."

Sammy nodded. His task wasn't to worry about his dad, but to get to second so he could kill the chance of a double play. Taking a long lead off first, he intentionally drew a throw and trotted back. He wanted to see the difference between the pitcher's throw from a stretch to first and his throw to home. The guy pitched with a definite rhythm that made him easy to read. On a one-and-one fastball to Trip, Sammy had a good lead and saw the pitcher committing to his smooth pitching motion. He ran and slid into second. The catcher scrambled to his feet but didn't bother throwing.

"Yo, Sir Speedy!" Gus yelled from the dugout.

Sammy smiled but quickly focused back on the game. Trip popped the next pitch into left field for an out. It was too close for Sammy to tag, and he stayed at second.

Danny came to the plate while Sammy mentally ran down the advantages of stealing third. Since Danny batted right-handed, that meant the catcher would have to throw around him. There was one out, so if he did get tagged it wouldn't end the inning. And once on third, he'd have lots of ways to score—a balk, an infield hit, a wild pitch. Being down one run, a score would tie the game. He decided it was worth the risk.

Sidestepping to his right, Sammy took a big lead. The pitcher eyed him and threw to the second baseman, but Sammy easily got back. As soon as the pitcher again turned his back, Sammy stepped into the same long lead. During the pitcher's next release, Sammy sprinted for third and slid. The catcher's throw was late and high. Sammy was safe. He'd stolen third.

More boisterous cheers flowed from the dugout as Sammy stood and brushed the dirt off his uniform. Stealing two bases in a row wasn't something he did every day. He couldn't help looking into the stands. His dad's arms were crossed as he nodded at something Mr. Jamison said, probably, "I thought your boy was a power hitter. What happened?"

Sammy frowned. Base running wasn't making him a slugger. It was just . . . running bases. He thought of Danny racing back for that obvious home run yesterday, acting like a show-off. Was that what Sammy was doing? Showing off to cover up for his lousy hitting?

Danny ended his at bat by striking out. Zack singled to right, sending Sammy home to tie the score. The inning then ended on Nick's pop fly.

Even though Wash said, "Nice job," when Sammy trotted over the plate, Sammy couldn't help thinking that a solo home run would have had the same result for a lot less work, *and* an RBI.

# CHAPTER *15*

Sammy's next two trips to the plate were at least no lousier than anyone else's, but that didn't make him feel better. He made sure to avoid eye contact with his dad as he headed to and from the outfield.

The score was still tied one apiece going into the top of the ninth. The Roadrunners took the field. Carson had been so sharp all game that Sammy's only defense had been chasing a foul ball in the fourth and a base hit in the sixth. The top of the Bulldogs' order was up. The first batter singled to center. A sacrifice bunt sent the runner to second. Then a double to deep left scored a run. Suddenly the Dogs were ahead two to one, with a man on second and one out.

It was obvious that Carson was tiring. But with one of the Runners' biggest financial backers watching his son's performance, Coach wouldn't pull the pitcher until he absolutely had to. He'd let Carson try to get out of the inning and impress the scouts with a complete game.

The Bulldogs' bulked-up slugger came to the plate. Sammy pounded his glove, twitchy and alert. After a meeting on the mound with Nick, Carson seemed to pull himself together and threw a couple of strikes. But on a two-and-two count, the batter blasted a drive into the right alley—the same location he'd hit his home run. But this one would drop.

Sammy had a good jump on the ball and waved off Danny. It was sinking fast, looking like a sure base hit, possibly a double.

Sammy's head told him to run back to the wall and snag it on a bounce. But his instincts told him he had a chance. Sprinting faster, he dove for the grass, his body and glove extended. Somersaulting to his feet, Sammy held up his glove. The white curve of the ball peeked out.

The Bulldogs' base runner must have figured it was a base hit, because he hadn't tagged up. As he scrambled to get back to second base, Sammy fired. Zack nailed the runner at second for a double play and the third out of the inning.

Danny slapped Sammy's arm with his glove as they trotted toward the dugout. "Great play, man."

"Thanks." Sammy was still breathing hard, the adrenaline pumping.

A few yards from the dugout, Danny said, "Hey, that rep is here. From the college I told you about? I just spotted him. None of us are showing what we can do with the bats. We need to be in the final tomorrow and get another chance."

Sammy grabbed Danny's arm. "Hold up." They stopped. "What are you saying?"

Danny shrugged. "Nothing. Just that we need to win this game."

"No, what I think you're saying is that you want me to start hitting and get us a win like I always do." Sammy's adrenaline was turning to anger. His face was on fire. "The last time I checked, there were eight other players on this team besides me. If you want to win, then do it! No one's stopping you!"

His team members gaped at him from the dugout. Sammy glared back. "All of you! Get off my back!"

Before barging into the dugout, he glanced into the stands. His dad's mouth hung open and his eyes were wide, like Sammy had just yelled at *him*. Marching back to the locker room, Sammy hurled his glove across the floor. His head felt like it would explode. He pressed his hands against his temples.

"Sammy." Coach Harris stood in the entrance to the dugout, his arms crossed.

"I'm sorry, okay?" Sammy said. "For yelling, for being me, for *whatever*!"

Coach uncrossed his arms and said quietly, "That was a great play out there. I don't know what's going on, but get your head together. You're batting fourth."

Sammy pounded his bare fist against a locker. Embarrassing himself at the plate again was the last thing he wanted to do. He was still angry, but now at himself. He wanted to sneak out of the ballpark and pretend this tournament never happened. But he had one more at-bat. If he could salvage something, even a base hit . . .

Sammy shook his head and laughed at himself. All he was hoping for was a *base hit*? That sucked. It *completely* sucked. He was a power hitter! He knew he could do this.

Grabbing his batting glove and helmet, Sammy strode to the dugout. Gus was batting, which meant Darius was already out. "Come on, Gus!" Sammy yelled, leaning against the railing. "Hit something!"

Gus was in his stance, staring at the pitcher. He swung. *Crack.* The ball skittered past the diving shortstop and into left field. Gus grinned at Sammy as he trotted to first base.

"Way to go!" Sammy yelled. He grabbed his bat and took Nellie's place on deck. Looping on a couple of weights, he took some hard practice swings.

Nellie quickly hit a pop foul to the third baseman. As he returned to the dugout, he said to Sammy, "What you said to Danny is right. It's not your responsibility to win for us."

"Yes, it is," Sammy replied. "This is my job." He stepped into the batter's box.

"Let's go, Sammy," Wash called from the coach's box. "You know what to do."

"Send me home, man!" Gus yelled from first base.

The dugout was quiet. Then Nellie broke the ice with, "Hit it, Sammy." Then his teammates erupted with, "Come on, Sammy!" "Slug it over the fence!" "Blast it!"

The Runners were down one run in the bottom of the ninth, with one man on and two outs. This was exactly where Sammy wanted to be. More than anyplace else on earth. Tapping the base twice, he raised the stick over his shoulder. His hands were dry in his gloves as he gripped the handle. He breathed evenly, watching the Bulldogs' pitcher shake his head at the catcher's first sign. Then the pitcher nodded. Winding up, he extended, and Sammy watched the ball leave the pitcher's hand.

The fastball floated, a little off, a little inside, just below the letters. Sammy could sense the pitcher wishing he could take it back. *Too late*, Sammy thought. *It's mine.* He swung with everything he had.

*CRACK!*

Sammy knew something was wrong the second he made contact.

# CHAPTER 16

The bat was suddenly too light, the follow-through too fast. Sammy saw two objects fly through the air at once: the ball toward deep center field and the end of his bat heading to third base. It happened so suddenly, the third baseman wasn't able to jump out of the way. The shard of wood sank deep into his upper thigh. He fell to the ground, screaming.

Horrified, Sammy raced onto the field, the first person to reach him. "I'm sorry!" He cradled the guy's head in his hands. Sammy looked over at Coach, still near the third-base box. "Get the EMTs!"

The third baseman was panting and grabbing at his leg. "God, it hurts."

Players from both teams crowded around. "Holy crap," one of them said when he saw the bloody shard sticking out of the player's leg.

"Shut up and give him some room," Sammy said. Then to the injured player he said, "You're gonna be okay. Take some deep breaths."

Sammy felt a pat on his shoulder. It was an emergency tech. "We've got him now."

Sammy gently lowered the player's head and backed up to give the emergency crew room to work. But Sammy didn't leave. He knew it wasn't his fault, but it was his bat and his swing.

"You okay?" Gus stood next to him.

"I think so," Sammy said. "I can't believe this. Those stupid bats."

Carson walked up to them and froze at the sight of the injured player. "Crap," he muttered. He glanced defensively at Sammy. "Aluminum bats are still more dangerous."

"I know," Sammy said, thinking of TJ.

Sammy's quick agreement seemed to catch Carson off guard. He took a deep breath and said, "Thanks for saving my complete game, even if it was a loss."

Sammy shrugged, his version of *you're welcome*. The pitcher turned on his heels and strode away. Sammy smiled to himself, knowing that was the closest they'd ever get to apologizing to each other.

Gus and Sammy waited together until the EMTs loaded the player into the ambulance, and then they headed for the dugout.

"I didn't even see what happened with my hit," Sammy said.

"The center fielder caught it about midfield."

"So even if my bat hadn't broken, I didn't hit it far enough."

Gus shrugged. "Sorry, amigo."

Up ahead, Sammy's dad stood near home plate talking to a short, middle-aged man

Sammy hadn't seen before. The guy saw
Sammy, waved, and walked toward him.

Gus said, "Uh oh, looks like trouble, dude.
I'll see you in the locker room." He slapped
Sammy's shoulder and left.

The man stuck his hand out. "Sammy
Perez?"

Sammy hesitated before shaking it. "Yeah."
Was this a cop? Was he going to arrest Sammy
for injuring the third baseman?

But the guy said, "I'm Chuck Engers,
scouting director for the San Diego Padres.
I've been watching you since your first game
yesterday."

"Oh. Sorry to disappoint you."

"Actually, you impressed the heck out of
me. With your base running and the way
you worked the pitcher yesterday. And that
incredible double steal and fielding play today.
You've got brains, speed, good instincts. And
you showed amazing poise taking care of that
injured player."

Sammy narrowed his eyes. "But I hardly
hit."

"How long have you been using wood?"

"Two weeks."

Engers laughed. "It takes time! Trust me. I've seen your stats. You'll improve." He stuck out his hand again and Sammy shook it. "I've got my eye on you, kid."

By now Sammy's dad had walked up and joined them. Engers shook his hand too. "Like I told you, Mr. Perez, you should be proud of your son. He's probably the most well-rounded talent at this tournament."

Engers walked off, leaving Sammy and his dad alone. Sammy took a deep breath. Between the game and the injury and now this scout, he felt hyped up and exhausted at the same time.

"Sammy," his dad said quietly, "I *am* proud of you. It's been so long since I've seen you play, I didn't know you have so many skills. By the end of the game I realized you're not the same as me. I was a power hitter, but you're a lot more than that. And I didn't need a scout to point it out to me."

"Thanks."

Sammy's dad lowered his voice, "And I'm canceling that doctor's appointment. It's not worth it. If you were all bulked up, there's no way you could have made that ballerina grab in the outfield today."

Sammy smiled and nodded.

"Good. Well, I need to drive Jamison to the airport. See you at home, champ."

. . .

By the time Sammy made it to the locker room, only Gus and Wash remained.

"You did good, Sammy," Wash said on his way out. "By the way, if you want me to keep helping you with wooden bats, I will."

Sammy nodded.

Gus sat on the bench next to Sammy as he gathered his things. "This was some tournament. Quite the emotional roller coaster. I'm thinking when we get home we should have an evening of entertainment."

Sammy paused, and then said, "Okay."

"Okay? I don't have to argue with you?"

"Nope. You and Olivia and me and Kelsey. Something totally unrelated to baseball."

Gus grinned. *"Muy bien,* man."

## ABOUT THE AUTHOR

M. G. Higgins writes fiction for children and young adults. Her nonfiction books (written under the name Melissa Higgins) range from biographies to self-help. She has loved baseball since she went to her first Dodgers' game at the age of six. Ms. Higgins can be found online at www.mghiggins.com.

"The road to the pros starts here."

LOOK FOR THESE
TITLES FROM THE
*TRAVEL TEAM*
COLLECTION.

# THE CATCH

When Danny makes "the catch," everyone seems interested in him. Girls text him, kids ask for autographs, and his highlight play even makes it on SportsCenter's Top Plays. A sports-gear executive tempts Danny with a big-money offer, and he decides to take advantage of his newfound fame. Danny agrees to wear the company's gear when he plays. But as his bank account gets bigger, so does his ego. Will Danny be able to keep his head in the game?

# POWER HITTER

Sammy Perez has to make it to the big leagues. After his teammate's career-ending injury, the Roadrunners decided to play in a wood bat tournament to protect their pitchers. And while Sammy used to be a hotheaded, hard-hitting, home-run machine, he's now stuck in the slump of his life. Sammy thinks the wood bats are causing the problem, but his dad suggests that maybe he's not strong enough. Is Sammy willing to break the law and sacrifice his health to get an edge by taking performance-enhancing drugs? Can Sammy break out of his slump in time to get noticed by major-league scouts?

# FORCED OUT

Zack Waddell's baseball IQ makes him one of the Roadrunners' most important players. When a new kid, Dustin, immediately takes their starting catcher's spot, Zack is puzzled. Dustin doesn't have the skills to be a starter. So Zack offers to help him with his swing in Dustin's swanky personal batting cages.

Zack accidentally overhears a conversation and figures out why Dustin is starting—and why the team is suddenly able to afford an expensive trip to a New York tournament. Will Zack's baseball instincts transfer off the field? Will the Roadrunners be able to stay focused when their team chemistry faces its greatest challenge yet?

# THE PROSPECT

Nick Cosimo eats, breathes, and lives baseball. He's a place-hitting catcher, with a cannon for an arm and a calculator for a brain. Thanks to his keen eye, Nick is able to pick apart his opponents, taking advantage of their weaknesses. His teammates and coaches rely on his good instincts between the white lines. But when Nick spots a scout in the stands, everything changes. Will Nick alter his game plan to impress the scout enough to get drafted? Or will Nick put the team before himself?

# OUT OF CONTROL

Carlos "Trip" Costas is a fiery shortstop with many talents and passions. His father is Julio Costas—yes, *the* Julio Costas, the famous singer. Unfortunately, Julio is also famous for being loud, controlling, and sometimes violent with Trip. Julio dreams of seeing his son play in the majors, but that's not what Trip wants.

When Trip decides to take a break from baseball to focus on his own music, his father loses his temper. He threatens to stop donating money to the team. Will the Roadrunners survive losing their biggest financial backer and their star shortstop? Will Trip have the courage to follow his dreams and not his father's?

# HIGH HEAT

Pitcher Seth Carter had Tommy John surgery on his elbow in hopes of being able to throw harder. Now his fastball cuts through batters like a 90 mph knife through butter. But one day, Seth's pitch gets away from him. The *clunk* of the ball on the batter's skull still haunts Seth in his sleep and on the field. His arm doesn't feel like part of his body anymore, and he goes from being the ace everybody wanted to the pitcher nobody trusts. With the biggest game of the year on the line, can Seth come through for the team?

# SOUTHSIDE HIGH

# ARE YOU A SURVIVOR?

check out all the books in the

# SURVIVING SOUTH SIDE

collection.

## Bad Deal

Fish hates having to take ADHD meds. They help him concentrate but also make him feel weird. So when a cute girl needs a boost to study for tests, Fish offers her one of his pills. Soon more kids want pills, and Fish likes the profits. To keep from running out, Fish finds a doctor who sells phony prescriptions. But suddenly the doctor is arrested. Fish realizes he needs to tell the truth. But will that cost him his friends?

## Recruited

Kadeem is a star quarterback for Southside High. He is thrilled when college scouts seek him out. One recruiter even introduces him to a college cheerleader and gives him money to have a good time. But then officials start to investigate illegal recruiting. Will Kadeem decide to help their investigation, even though it means the end of the good times? What will it do to his chances of playing in college?

## Benito Runs

Benito's father had been in Iraq for over a year. When he returns, Benito's family life is not the same. Dad suffers from PTSD—post-traumatic stress disorder—and yells constantly. Benito can't handle seeing his dad so crazy, so he decides to run away. Will Benny find a new life? Or will he learn how to deal with his dad—through good times and bad?

## PLAN B

Lucy has her life planned: She'll graduate and join her boyfriend at college in Austin. She'll become a Spanish teacher, and of course they'll get married. So there's no reason to wait, right? They try to be careful, but Lucy gets pregnant. Lucy's plan is gone. How will she make the most difficult decision of her life?

## BEATEN

Keah's a cheerleader and Ty's a football star, so they seem like the perfect couple. But when they have their first fight, Ty is beginning to scare Keah with his anger. Then after losing a game, Ty goes ballistic and hits Keah repeatedly. Ty is arrested for assault, but Keah still secretly meets up with Ty. How can Keah be with someone she's afraid of? What's worse—flinching every time your boyfriend gets angry or being alone?

## Shattered Star

Cassie is the best singer at Southside and dreams of being famous. She skips school to try out for a national talent competition. But her hopes sink when she sees the line. Then a talent agent shows up, and Cassie is flattered to hear she has "the look" he wants. Soon she is lying and missing rehearsal to meet with him. And he's asking her for more each time. How far will Cassie go for her shot at fame?